THE FALLOW AND THE FAINT

CURSED: ECHO

OTHER BOOKS

Fated

The Head and the Heart

The Flower and the Flame

The Sorrow and the Sea

Cursed

The Princess and the Prophecy

The Fallow and the Faint

The Weaver and the Web

THE FALLOW AND THE FAINT

CURSED: ECHO

KERRI KEBERLY

Dragonfire Press

Print ISBN: 978-1-958354-80-3

CHAPTER 1

ECHO GIGGLED, PEEKING from her hiding spot before ducking low in the brush. She was one of the many mountain nymphs whose favorite pastime was to frolic in the forest groves and sparkling streams of Mount Cithaeron. Among them, her feet were the lightest and her laughter the most cheerful.

Like all nymphs, she was beautiful, with fair hair and eyes as clear and blue as a cloudless sky, but she was known for her storytelling best of all. Echo could capture one's attention with her comeliness and grace, to be sure, but she could hold it with her spellbinding words. It was a gift she used often, for she delighted in making others smile.

Echo squeaked when she felt a light tap on one shoulder.

"You really must find somewhere new to hide, Echo," laughed Aethra.

Echo wheeled around to see her sister standing above her with her fists planted on her hips in mock reprimand. Echo could not stop a peal of laughter from escaping when she jumped to her feet and threw her arms around her sister's shoulders.

It was like that sometimes; the joy bubbling within her could simply not be contained.

"We all know I'm better with words," replied Echo, grabbing Aethra by the hand. "Come, let's find Eudora, so the three of us can pay the goddesses a visit. You can play the lyre while I entertain them with a story."

Echo and Aethra tip-toed through the grove, careful not to crush the tiny, yellow-petaled buttercups underfoot as they searched for Eudora. They headed toward the stream gurgling in the distance, stopping to smell every patch of fragrant primrose along the way.

Echo smiled when she caught a flash of red locks through a thick grove of saplings.

"Over there," she whispered to Aethra, pointing in the direction in which she'd seen Eudora.

They carefully made their way toward the beacon of pale skin and ginger tresses in the dappled light undulating through the leaves, without making any sound at all.

As they got closer, Echo could see Eudora was standing at the base of an enormous oak, her gaze fixed upward. She pressed a finger to her lips, signaling for Aethra to remain stealthy. As they crept forward, Echo could now see that Eudora's ivory skin bore the barest hint of pink. It was obvious by the way she nervously shifted her weight from one delicate foot to the other that something high in the thick branches had caught her attention.

When Eudora's lips began to move, it was clear it was some*one* and not some*thing*.

"Who is she talking to?" whispered Aethra.

"I don't know," Echo whispered back. "A satyr, perhaps?"

Echo knew as soon as the words made their way out of her mouth it was an impossibility. Satyrs could speak, yes, but their cloven feet could not climb trees. No, it had to be a more powerful divinity to whom Eudora spoke.

Artemis visited these mountain woods from time to time.

Echo's stomach looped with the sudden fear Eudora had somehow offended the goddess of the hunt and was now trying to talk her way out of trouble. Like all goddesses, Artemis was benevolent when at peace, but break her trust or raise her ire and she could become viciously cruel in her punishment.

Echo's mind raced for what soothing words would calm the goddess enough to untangle her sister from a dangerous web, should she need to.

A gasp came from Aethra, and Echo saw to whom Eudora was speaking a moment later.

Zeus lounged high within the tree, leaning against the thick trunk with one knee up while the other hung off the enormous branch where he sat, swinging ever so slightly. His hair was long and loose, the ends lifting in the crisp mountain breeze. Smooth, high cheekbones gave way to a beard surrounding full lips that held a languid smile.

What was the king of the gods doing in the woods? Perched in a tree, at that.

Echo swallowed hard when his piercing gaze, as blue as the deepest mountaintop spring, turned toward her and Aethra, who both stood stunned.

Echo reached out, pulling Aethra down into a curtsey and then bowing deeply herself. When they rose, he was grinning broadly at them.

"Beautiful day is it not, my ladies?" he said, gesturing toward the sky before cupping his knee casually. The bottom of his tunic had settled into the crease of his hip, revealing a muscular upper thigh.

Echo blinked. This was no time to be lost in stupor.

"A lovely day, indeed," she said, smiling brightly. "What brings you down from mighty Olympus to our humble little mountain, Your Majesty?"

Eudora shot Echo a side-long look. Her sister's lips were pushed out into the slightest pout, indicating she was irritated by the interruption.

"Why, what else?" He inhaled, as if to prove it was truly the bracing mountain air he sought. "I came down for a bit of time to myself, and just so happened upon your lovely sister."

Echo continued to smile politely, even though she knew the truth. Zeus's quest had nothing to do with admiring the beauty of field and stream, and everything to do with ogling the nymphs who dwelled among them.

But she dared not call out the king of the gods for his true intentions.

"It's no wonder," said Echo, switching her gaze to Eudora, "She is the loveliest of us all." She stepped toward her sister, intent on pulling her away. "But it's time for us to entertain the goddesses, and so she must be going."

Echo's fingertips brushed the soft bare skin of Eudora's arm just as she stepped out of reach.

"I do not wish to be rude to His Majesty," said Eudora, glancing up at Zeus. "Do go on without me. I'm sure the goddesses will not even notice my absence."

A ghost of a smile tipped Zeus's lips. "Yes, do go on without Eudora," he said. "I shall make sure no harm befalls her, for I quite like her company."

Echo looked back at Aethra with arched brows, but she got no answer to her silent question, and so she tried a final time. The goddesses, especially Zeus's wife, Hera, noticed everything.

Echo cleared her throat, aiming to work her magic, but before she could get the words out, Zeus spoke.

"Go now," said Zeus. His tone was not harsh, but there was no mistaking it was the end of the discussion. Eudora would not be going anywhere. "And be sure to entertain them with a very, *very* long story, Echo."

CHAPTER 2

Eager to impress the goddesses who dwelled among the highest peak of Mount Olympus, Echo and Aethra hurried along the rocky path that led to the palace high in the clouds. Aphrodite was the first to greet them when they arrived, breathless and pink-cheeked.

The goddess led them to a garden veranda, where columns lined the edges, with billowing diaphanous curtains swaying in the breeze, and an enormous fountain gurgling in the center.

"Gather round, sisters," Aphrodite called out, "the oreads Aethra and Echo are here to entertain us."

Once all were settled on cushioned stools and reclining couches, Echo nodded to Aethra, indicating she was ready to begin. No one had commented on Eudora's absence, yet Echo's pulse jumped. Despite her nerves, she smiled sweetly at the goddesses gathered round—Hestia, Demeter, and Aphrodite—as Aethra strummed a soothing melody on the lyre.

Echo spun her story, creating a scene so colorful and vivid, the goddesses sat rapt, listening intently to every word. The stories she told were always about one of them going on an adventure, saving the day by puzzling out a riddle and imparting wisdom, or falling in love—sometimes all three. Today's tale took inspiration from Aphrodite and her ability to inspire love and lust in mortals as well as gods, and of course, this elicited delighted smiles and excited claps from the exuberant goddess.

Even Hera, who was sitting close by but pretending not to be interested, was leaning an ear closer so that she could eavesdrop. The more the queen of the gods tried to seem inconspicuous, the louder Echo spoke. When she could see Hera was practically falling over with anticipation, she lowered her voice, hoping that whispering the finale with an arched brow would cause Hera to join them. But the queen was too prideful for that, and remained seated apart from the others, even when the other goddesses broke out in a round of applause once the story was finished.

Echo bit the inside of her lip at Hera's stubbornness. The only thing to ever move Hera to action was her husband. How many stories could Echo tell before Hera grew weary and sent them away?

"Come now, Echo," said Aphrodite, laughing softly. "Don't be vexed. As always, you've told a wonderful story. We all enjoyed it, didn't we?"

Hestia and Demeter nodded in agreement, also mistaking the source of Echo's worry.

"Oh, yes, your stories are always so wonderful," said Hestia, leaning forward on her stool, eager for another to begin.

Echo smoothed her furrowed brow. The misunderstanding, though unfortunate, was the perfect way to keep the conversation going. She needed to keep Hera from getting up and wandering away, leaving her mind unoccupied and free to wonder where—or with who—her husband was currently spending his day. What would draw in the goddess of family more than the mention of marriage?

Echo cleared her throat before Aethra could start another song.

"May I ask you a question?" she began, turning toward Aphrodite and speaking loudly enough for Hera to hear. "About marriage."

"Of course," replied Aphrodite. "What is it you'd like to know?"

Echo saw Hera stiffen out of the corner of her eye and had to resist the urge to smile at her accomplishment. It was evident Hera found asking the goddess of love and lust about marriage and fidelity was preposterous.

"What makes a marriage happy?" The question was simple, and Echo could already guess the answer, but it had done what it was intended to do. Hera now gazed directly at them, head tilted, one eyebrow arched with anticipation.

Hera's open interest did not go unnoticed by Aphrodite. She glanced at the queen of the gods before answering. "There are many things required to make a marriage happy."

Satisfied, Hera gave a slight nod before turning her head away. Having placated her powerful fellow goddess, a half-smile pushed up the corner of Aphrodite's mouth.

"Is there a satyr for whom you pine?" she continued, sitting up straight as she returned her gaze to Echo.

Echo giggled nervously. "Oh, no. I was simply..." She glanced at Hera. "Wondering."

"About which, love or lust?" replied Aphrodite. "Satyrs are naturally salacious creatures, you know, but I can command whichever one of them you desire to be filled with as much abiding love for you as you wish."

Echo's eyes went wide, trying to imagine possessing such power. It seemed impossible that she could have romantic feelings toward anyone, mortal or satyr. She had never encountered a mortal to know, but she couldn't imagine they'd stir any more feelings of love or lust in her than a satyr could. The only love Echo had ever known was platonic, and it was for the goddesses and her sisters.

But she did not want to disappoint Aphrodite, and so, for Eudora's sake, she continued as though she were truly interested. According to the flush of her sister's skin and the breathiness of her speech when they had been in the company of Zeus, Eudora was quite capable of feeling romantic love.

Or was it simply lust her sister was experiencing?

Either way, if Eudora continued down the path she was currently on, it would not bode well for her. The nymph Callisto was proof of that. Rumor had it she still roamed the woods of Arcadia as a bear.

Echo's belly flipped at the thought. She would not let such a terrible thing befall her sweet Eudora.

"How does one tell the difference between the two?" asked Echo. "Love and lust, I mean."

"Well, both bring great pleasure," began Aphrodite. "True, they can sometimes feel the same, but one sets the heart alight and the other sets the loins afire." She sent Echo a mischievous smile. "Which do you seek to be impassioned by, dear one?"

Echo opened her mouth to speak, but with a swish of fabric, Hera was standing before them, finally spurred into action.

"Stop filling this nymph's head with your silly whims of fancy, Aphrodite," said Hera. She set her emerald gaze upon Echo, who shrank under its weight. "When your heart beats wild with longing, that is when you lust. When it breaks so fiercely you scarcely think you can go on, that is love."

Aphrodite scoffed, offended at Hera's jaded view on love and lust, but before she could articulate her displeasure and issue a rebuttal, Hera turned on her heel and walked away.

CHAPTER 3

AS THEY DID every morning, Echo, Aethra, and Eudora had gathered on the mountaintop to watch the sunrise. On their way back down to the stream, Echo relayed all that she had learned about love and lust to Eudora.

She had been on the verge of telling her how Hera had given her opinion on the difference, when the birds flitting about began to chirp and carry on so loudly, they nearly drowned out Echo's voice completely. Normally, she delighted in the sweet and cheerful songs they sang, but this morning, her lips pursed in frustration at their voracious warbling. Irritation crumpled her brow. It was her duty as an older sister to warn Eudora about the dangers of consorting with Zeus.

"What did you and Zeus talk about yesterday, Eudora?" asked Aethra, forcing the conversation before Echo was ready. For the first time in her life, she wanted to throttle Aethra, but the mention of Zeus had quieted the birds, and so Echo refrained from scolding her sister for interrupting. Instead, she narrowed her eyes at the sky.

Could the abrupt ceasing of birdsong be the work of the lusty god who ruled over it? Had he sent the tiny, yellow- and red-breasted creatures to interfere, so that Eudora would hear not a single word of warning?

"He told me of how he rescued his siblings from his father," replied Eudora.

"And that was all?" prodded Echo.

"He also told me of the battle between the Titans, and how he and the Olympians won, casting the worst of Gaia's children down into Tartarus. To which I thanked him for seeing to it we had such a tranquil mountain home to dwell. Nothing inappropriate, if that is what you wish to know."

Her words seemed guileless enough, with no hint of deception. Was there a chance the encounter truly was innocent, and that Eudora may not need to be cautioned? Everyone knew how jealous Hera could be when it came to her husband's conquests. Eudora must have known it would have behooved her not to encourage Zeus if she did not want to end up a babbling brook, or worse, a boulder, one that's only attractive feature was that it was a broad enough spot to sit.

Relieved, Echo decided she would proceed with a cautionary tale only if necessary. But when she looked up at the surrounding trees, her lips pressed into a thin line at what she saw. It seemed her suspicions might be founded. It was possible the king of the gods may have sent the birds to hinder and distract, for they followed behind her and her sisters like moths to a flame, flying from tree to tree as they made their way along the well-worn path.

"You sing so lovely, Eudora," said Echo. "I'm sure the goddesses missed you."

"I... I..." stammered Eudora. "Well, I suppose they may have—"

"You should come with us next time," said Aethra.

Eudora's cheeks grew as rosy as pomegranates at the suggestion. "You would have me offend the king of the gods, then?"

Echo's already fading smile disappeared completely, leaving a frown in its place. Her gaze met Aethra's, whose worried expression mirrored her own. Eudora's true feelings had finally come to the surface, confirming Echo must indeed dissuade her sister from seeking the favor of Zeus.

She sighed, looking back at her sweet but naïve younger sister. It was evident Eudora was already smitten beyond reproach. The task of warning her would be difficult enough, but

Echo would need to speak in riddles to fool the squawking little spies Zeus had sent, having to raise her voice just to be heard.

Two things she tried never to do.

"Have you heard of the story of Io?" began Echo. "Turned into a cow by Zeus so that his wife Hera would not discover the love affair—"

"Do not regale me with a cleverly disguised admonition, Echo," cut in Eudora. "Zeus honors me, a lowly mountain nymph, with his time, nothing more, and I quite enjoy our conversations."

"You've had more than one?" said Aethra, eyes going wide.

Echo's heart pounded in her chest. She'd caught the slip as well. Just how long had Eudora been meeting with Zeus?

"Yes!" cried Eudora. "And I will have a thousand more if he wishes it so."

Echo opened her mouth to speak, but before she could utter a single word, a deep and divine voice filled the surrounding forest with its rich and resounding timbre.

"I hear the goddesses were quite entertained with your stories, Echo."

All three of them gasped, stopping in their tracks when Zeus appeared, leaning on a tree up ahead of them, grinning from ear to ear.

Echo bowed her head, heart firmly lodging in her throat. Embarrassment kissed her cheeks with its flame while her mind raced to find the words to appease the god before them. It seemed she did not need them, however.

"There is no need for that," said Zeus. "Think of me as you would any man when I am here." He gestured to the tall cedars and rocky cliffs surrounding them. "I come to appreciate the beauty of this place, and all who call it home. I cannot help but be grateful, for I was raised by the nymph Amalthea." He held out his hand. "Come, let us four find a place to sit, and I will tell you about my time among the nymphs of Crete."

Echo resisted the urge to frown, offering Zeus a placid smile instead. His intentions seemed pure, and she was all for a good story, but how could she know for sure his sweet and patronizing talk wasn't something all men did. According to the virgin goddess of the hunt, Artemis, it was, and nymphs should steer clear of them.

Indecision warred within Echo. It was in her nature to please those around her, often at the expense of her own comfort, but, up until now, it had been all nymphs and goddesses. What made women happy was so much easier to figure out, yet she found herself not wanting to disappoint a god, and not just any god. Zeus was ruler over them all, the one who had fought the titans and won, so that she and her sisters could call this mountain home.

Zeus had no sooner finished speaking when Eudora rushed toward him, accepting his invitation without a second thought. Echo looked at Aethra. Her eyes were round and full of admiration now, too.

"What harm could there be in listening?" said Aethra, shrugging.

Echo gnawed on her lip. For once, she didn't know what to do, but even more cause for alarm, she didn't know what to say.

Aethra nodded once, making Echo's decision for her.

"I'll watch over her. You keep the goddesses occupied," instructed Aethra before darting away and catching up to Eudora.

CHAPTER 4

AFTER WATCHING THE sun rise alone, Echo walked along the path to the stream. The morning was crisp, with dew still coating the leaves. The birds in the treetops sang to the squirrels below, who foraged along the forest floor.

It had been several days since her and her sisters' encounter with Zeus. Though she had waited for them each morning, she had not seen hide nor hair of her sisters, and she was beginning to worry.

She sighed heavily as she walked along. What should she do? She would continue to look for Aethra and Eudora, yes, but how would she explain their long absence? They went to the mountain often. Surely, the goddesses would question a fortnight with no music, no singing, and no stories to delight them.

A faint laugh floated on the breeze, causing Echo's heart to take flight. It had nowhere to go, and so it remained in her chest, throwing itself against her ribcage in a desperate attempt to break free.

The sound carried up from somewhere below, barely audible over the rushing of water. Echo made her way through a dome of cedar trees, letting the laughter guide her as she pushed aside the fragrant branches. The mirth came freely and unabashedly, and then someone began to play the lyre. A moment later, a melody, high and sweet, rang out. There were no words, but the sound of it made Echo gnaw at her bottom lip. She knew that voice anywhere, as well as the lyre playing that accompanied it.

Her brow furrowed as she slowly approached the edge of a waterfall. She knew who she would see them cavorting with, and it saddened her. It had been her who had made them sit wide-eyed and still with her stories. This time, Echo feared, her sisters were not laughing at some silly made-up tale of goddesses or heroes. This time, they were utterly transfixed by every word that came out of Zeus's mouth.

Echo could not see why. He spoke so blatantly, with no tact or subtlety. She would admit he was pleasing to look at, with hair covering his broad chest, flowing locks, and a thick beard. He was brawnier than most, even Ares, the god of war. In truth, he reminded her of an enormous bear. Being the father of such a hot-tempered and blood thirsty warrior as Ares, she supposed he might lash out as viciously as one when provoked.

She stepped lightly, carefully placing one foot in front of the other until she came to a tree hanging over the very edge of the waterfall. She stood beside its grooved and leaning trunk, steadying herself before inhaling deeply and peering down at the sparkling pool below.

Her heart sank at what she saw. She knew she would find her sisters there with the god, but she had not expected to see so much of their modesty discarded.

It seemed Eros had seen to it that both her sisters were lovestruck.

Zeus floated in the crystal water naked, his face warmed by the sun as the tranquil rippling and soothing melodies washed over him. Her sisters were barely dressed, their breasts and thighs bared as they played for him.

What kind of stories had he told for them to act so familiar with one another?

Echo stared with wide eyes at her sisters, wondering what it felt like to be so filled with desire one would brazenly cavort half naked around a man. She wasn't against the workings of Aphrodite. It was simply that no one had ever stirred this sort of bravery within her.

Suddenly, water splashed over her sisters. Their playing stopped and their giggling began anew as the droplets rained down upon them. Echo flinched, her gaze cutting to Zeus. He was smiling broadly and beckoning Aethra and Eudora to join him. Echo's mouth dropped open when, without hesitation, her sisters shed what remained of their clothing and dove into the sparkling blue water. Eudora swam like a naiad into Zeus's awaiting arms, and when Aethra broke the surface behind him, she threw her arms around his shoulders, pressing her breasts against his smooth, broad back before laying her flushed cheek against the back of his head.

Echo gasped, her hand flying to her mouth when, without prompting, Eudora offered her neck to Zeus, whose lips hungrily accepted. Her mind raced, though not with wonton thoughts. She was not such a prude that she would deny her sisters their pleasure.

No, she was trying to think of a way to protect them.

This waterfall was unknown to others; one among many cascading down within the mountain. Its remote location wasn't what made Echo's stomach tighten with unease, however. The question that gripped her with fear was how long before Hera took notice of not just Aethra and Eudora's absence, but Zeus's?

Should the jealous and vengeful goddess catch wind of their clandestine visits with her husband, it would be the end of Aethra and Eudora.

CHAPTER 5

ONCE ECHO WAS far enough away from the scene, she sprinted for Olympus like a doe running for her life. In truth, she was running for her sisters' lives, which made her legs move even faster, a blur streaking through the forest until she was at the base of the divine mountain.

She stopped to catch her breath, placing a hand on her chest to soothe her burning lungs. Or was it to calm her jittering heart? Either way, arriving alone would be suspicious enough, she did not need to enter the gardens panting like prey.

Echo climbed onto a nearby rock to wait until her breathing returned to normal. She lifted her hair, fanning her neck as she thought of the best way to capture Hera's attention. Whatever she came up with, her recital would need to be long and the details riveting to keep the notoriously fretful goddess distracted.

Echo's lips tipped into the faintest of smiles. She knew just the story to tell. It would take hours to finish, perhaps even days.

Skin cooled and sweat dried, Echo dropped her long tresses and slid down from the rock. When she spied several bunches of white lilies as she made her way along the path that led up to the mountain, she hurried to gather them. They were Hera's favorite. Echo would bring them as an offering to the goddess, for she would need all the help she could get to soften the hard-headed queen of the gods.

She also picked some primrose growing around a nearby grove of olive trees, lest the other goddesses be offended at receiving nothing. Hestia would remain gracious, Echo knew, but the same could not be said for Aphrodite, Demeter, or Artemis. Hopefully Athena would be too engaged in a battle of wits somewhere to even care, but Echo would bring olives as well, just in case.

Skirts full of flowers and fruit, Echo finally reached the top of the mountain. She pushed aside the hanging vines that led into the gardens with one hand, clutching the fabric of her dress she'd used as a basket in the other.

The verdant lushness of the gardens never failed to amaze Echo. She inhaled deeply, taking in the air, which, as impossible as it seemed, was even more invigorating than the air on her own mountain peak. It was no wonder. Gods and goddesses roamed here. These gardens were divine in nature, and an honor to be able to visit at will.

It did not take long for Aphrodite to greet Echo with a warm welcome.

"Is that primrose I smell?" murmured Aphrodite, the rose-gold aura that always surrounded her glowing brightly as she glided toward Echo.

"It is, and they are for you, my lady of love and desire," replied Echo, handing a bunch of the delicate flowers to the goddess. "I have something for all of you."

Aphrodite accepted the flowers, burying her nose into the fragrant blooms. "You are so thoughtful, dear one."

"Is Hera in the gardens this day?" asked Echo, trying not to seem too anxious. "I've brought her some lilies."

Aphrodite fluttered her lashes, putting forth no attempt to disguise her irritation at the switch in focus. "I believe I saw her earlier, sulking somewhere over there." She waved her hand absently toward a pond off in the distance, surrounded by weeping willows.

"Thank you." Echo nodded before rushing off to find the rest of the goddesses and give them their gifts. If she could not find them, she would leave the offerings at the base of their statues found throughout the gardens.

Echo left the olives by Athena's statue, and some of the primrose at the marble likeness of Artemis. After the task was done, she headed toward the small cottage where Hestia was found most often. It was quaint and charming, surrounded by colorful flowers with ivy covering the stone and a thin whisp of smoke curling up from the chimney. Echo thought it suited the goddess of hearth and home perfectly.

As expected, Hestia invited Echo in to sit with her and Demeter for a bit of freshly baked bread. Being the most even-tempered of the goddesses, both were gracious when Echo politely declined.

"I am honored, but I cannot stay. I must give these lilies to Hera before they wilt," she said, handing over the rest of the primrose. "These are for you and Demeter."

Hestia thanked her, smiling as she offered Echo a jar brimming with water—appearing with a wave of her hand—for Hera's lilies, even though they both knew the flowers would remain as lovely and fresh as the moment they were plucked. That was the way of Olympus.

Echo thanked her profusely before turning and rushing off toward the pond. A chorus of trilling frogs grew louder as she approached, as did the buzzing from a spotted odonatan's iridescent wings as it flew past her to land on the reeds swaying gently. Her heart sank when her gaze scoured the muddy banks and surrounding area but did not see Hera.

"Who dares disturb my peace?"

Echo flinched, barely suppressing a frightened squeak. She squinted in the direction from which Hera's voice had come. She saw an ancient looking weeping willow, its long branches hanging low and sweeping the ground. Echo clutched the lilies to her chest as she took a step toward the tree, its delicate leaves creating a living curtain, concealing whoever sought comfort within the tree's embrace.

"It is I, Echo," she replied, pushing aside the branches and stepping into what could only be described as a sanctuary.

Hera sat upon a cushioned reclining couch, clad in an indigo chiton and a circlet of gold sitting atop her glossy dark hair. A pair of peacocks roamed the perimeter while smaller birds—canaries, wrens, and finches—fluttered about. There was only one bird that was caged, a cuckoo, with its gilded prison hanging from high up in one of the branches. "The storyteller—"

"Ah yes, the nymph who indulges Aphrodite's vanity," said Hera quietly. "Who wishes to know of lust and love."

Strangely, Echo didn't know how to respond to the comment, and so she held the lilies out to the goddess instead. "These are for you, my lady."

Her breath caught when Hera turned her head and fixed bright green eyes upon her. How had she never noticed what a striking shade of peridot they were? Hera was every bit as breathtaking as Aphrodite, and Echo could not fathom why Zeus would ever stray from his queen.

She swallowed hard when the answer came to her. Lust, that was how. Was it any wonder why Hera had bristled at the mention of it? It was not love that drove her husband to forsake her time and time again, with mortals... goddesses...

Mountain nymphs.

Echo suppressed a shiver as she approached Hera, placing the jar of lilies in front of the couch before bowing low.

Echo looked up when Hera said, "My favorite."

Hera gave Echo a slight nod before gesturing toward a small table positioned next to the couch. When she glanced down into a golden amethyst encrusted chalice, Echo saw how the liquid inside shimmered with light, even in the shade.

The cuckoo bird let out a *ka-ka-ka-ka-ka-kow-kow-kowlp-kowlp-kowlp* as Echo placed the flowers on the table next to the chalice. Sadness clawed at her heart when she thought of how the male cuckoo's desperate call for a mate would be forever futile. Her stomach clenched when she remembered it was as a cuckoo Zeus had disguised himself to trick Hera into marriage.

"You are quite perceptive, Echo," said Hera. "What is it that you want?"

"Naught but your company, my lady," replied Echo. "I wondered if I might hear more regarding the subject of marriage. Or perhaps, if you find it bothersome to converse just now, I might entertain you with a story?"

If Hera allowed her to, she would retell the goddess's tale, and she would give it a happier ending.

CHAPTER 6

THOUGH HERA DIDN'T speak, Echo took the absence of a dismissal as permission to stay, and so she sat on the mossy ground with her legs folded beneath her and began to tell the goddess a story.

A long time ago, when order was born from chaos, the mother earth, Gaia, was formed. After a while, Gaia grew lonely for an equal, and so she brought forth Uranus, who quickly fell in love with her. He had been created to lay above and on all sides of her, and so he did. Soon the first Titans were born, among them, Rhea and Cronus, who, much like Gaia and Uranus, loved each other deeply. It was not long before the two would follow in the footsteps of heaven and earth and join as one.

Hera made a noise in her throat. "Rhea and Cronus, my mother and father," she said. "But we are not there yet, are we?"

Echo offered a comforting smile, shaking her head gently before continuing.

As time went on, Gaia and Uranus had many more children. Consumed with his desire for her, Uranus began to smother Gaia, hiding the next generation of their children within her. These children were immense and uncontrollable—some with fifty heads and an equal number of limbs—and caused Gaia great pain. Distraught, she devised a plan. She fashioned a sickle and called to her son Cronus...

Hera gazed absently through the swaying branches of the willow. Echo knew the goddess was no longer in her sanctuary but in her head, envisioning the long-ago scene Echo was setting.

The titan exacted his mother's revenge, of course, and from the blood spilled sprang the Erinyes, giants, and my cousins, the ash-tree nymphs.

"Don't forget Aphrodite, the goddess of lust," said Hera flatly. "Born from his genitals, which were cut off by my father and cast into the sea."

Echo had chosen her words carefully to avoid that detail. She pressed her lips together and cleared her throat.

Angered by his son's betrayal, Uranus revealed to Cronus that he would be overthrown by one of his own children.

Hera interrupted again. "So, he swallowed his first born, even though it was not a son, but a daughter."

Echo moved closer, reaching out and laying a hand over Hera's, which rested in her lap. Her skin was soft, but ice cold.

"Yes, and every child after that, until Rhea, cunning like her mother, devised a plan."

When her last child was born, she concealed him by sending him to far away Crete. She swaddled a stone in his stead, for she knew her husband would soon come to take the child away from her. Rhea handed over the bundle. Suspecting nothing, Cronus accepted it, and with no hesitation swallowed it.

Hera peered down at Echo, her unlined face a study of control. "He consumed five of us. Myself, Hestia, Demeter, Poseidon, and Hades."

"He did, my lady, but he was none the wiser when he left Rhea that day, smiling triumphantly knowing she had outwitted him and that her youngest son still lived," replied Echo.

Hera pulled her hand from beneath Echo's and leaned back. The chalice had disappeared from the table to reappear in Hera's hand. "A shame she was forced to deceive her husband in the first place, was it not?" She brought the cup to her lips for a sip of the golden nectar of the gods.

The cuckoo called out again, causing Echo's heart to stutter in her chest. She had chosen to tell the wrong story—she could see that now—but there was no turning back. She must not raise suspicion. She must finish what she started, proceeding with caution, careful not to open any more of Hera's wounds. Echo inhaled before assuming her former position and resumed the story.

Many years passed, and as the godling grew, the nymphs entrusted with his care kept nothing from him. He knew how much his mother had suffered at the hands of his father, who had savagely taken their children from her by eating them. It had been done out of fear, but that did not dampen his anger. The deed was unforgivable, and so he, too, devised a plan. When he came of age, and was strong enough, he would free them.

Hera's chin lifted ever so slightly, a look of pride flashing across her face before smoothing itself into an expression of stoicism once more. It made Echo wonder if it was the brazen young god who'd saved her that Hera fell in love with, or the powerful king he would become.

"When he had come of age, the god—" began Echo.

"You may speak his name, nymph," said Hera, taking another sip of nectar. "In fact, I prefer it."

Echo nodded, relieved. "When Zeus had come of age, he went to his father's palace disguised as a cupbearer."

"Clever. Wouldn't you agree?" said Hera.

Echo nodded, but instead of relief, an uncertainty now bubbled in the pit of her stomach. Hera's question held double meaning, and the hair on the back of Echo's neck rose when she realized with sudden clarity the caged bird was a stand-in for Zeus.

CHAPTER 7

ECHO HAD CHANGED positions, her arms now wrapped around her knees protectively, her heart jumping as she peered up at the goddess before her.

"And what of the daughters Cronus imprisoned?" asked Hera, tilting her head. When Echo dared not answer—the question was rhetorical—Hera continued. "I shall tell you."

They were grateful to be rescued, these daughters of Rhea. At first, there was no doubt in the eldest of them their savior had acted purely out of the kindness of his heart, exacting revenge on behalf of his siblings because he thought them equals. It soon came to pass, however, that justice had a price.

Echo could do was sit and listen. She bit the inside of her cheek, biding her time and waiting patiently for an opportunity to take back the reins.

It started with small gifts. She was flattered, of course, but it was only companionship she craved. Despite her refusals, his plying continued, and his advances became incessant.

As you might imagine, it did not take long for her to grow angry. Could he not see she was his elder, worthy of respect as such? Did he not understand virtue? She would not lay with a man unless they were joined as one through the bonds of matrimony.

And on it went, cat chasing mouse. When it became too much to bear, she would find refuge in the forest, seeking solace among the gentle woodland creatures. Birds were her favorite. Their songs comforted her, lifting her spirits until she was carefree once more.

Until one day, when she discovered one of them was injured. Her heart broke, bringing tears to her eyes to see it grounded, hopping around the forest floor with its wing broken and limp. She rushed over to the cuckoo, gently picking it up and cradling it to her breast.

"I told it not to worry, that I would fix its wing and that it would fly once more," said Hera, her nostrils flaring as she set her jaw, her eyes glittering with contempt.

Echo hugged her knees tighter. Though she had not been privy to the private details of Hera's story, she knew the moments the goddess was about to recount next would be horrifying. Echo resisted the urge to press her hands over her ears. She did not want to hear of the treachery done by Zeus and excused by all because he had become their king.

But she remained still, swallowing hard as Hera took a moment to compose herself.

The transformation happened so quickly, and his clutch held so firmly, there was no chance for her to flee...

Echo shrank in on herself, sadness and confusion swirling in her head and in her heart. This was not the story she wanted to hear, and it certainly was not the tale she'd intended to tell. How could she possibly reconcile the jovial god she'd met, the one who seemed to treat her sisters like cherished treasures, with Hera's version of him?

And when it was over, she had no choice but to accept his proposal of marriage. It was not as though she thought marriage to be undesirable, or that she could not eventually grow to love him, but more that she had been tricked into these things. Moreover, she did not want the others to know she was no longer virtuous. In truth, her virtue had been stolen, and the loss of it, despite her conviction to keep it safe, was too much for her to bear.

Echo unfolded her legs and scooted closer to Hera. "Will you tell me all there is to know about marriage, my lady?" She rested her elbows on the seat of the couch, placing her chin on her fingers. She donned an eager expression, hoping it would be enough to change course and stop Hera from reminiscing, or at least guide the goddess's mind to happier thoughts.

Hera looked down her nose at Echo with eyes full of bitterness and rage. Her green gaze flashed dangerously, her words more snarl than answer. "Marriage is sacred, a privilege, *an oath*. It is a vow to be honored and cherished, not taken lightly, do you understand?"

Scarcely able to breathe, Echo nodded. On the surface, the words themselves were harmless, but steeped in such venom, they were deadly. Even more frightening was how that poison seemed to be aimed at her. Frozen with fear, Echo regretted seeking out the queen of the gods at all.

She needed to say something, anything to calm Hera down, but before Echo could find her bearings, the goddess stood. She lifted her hand, the chalice appearing in time for it to meet her ruby lips for a sip. Except, she didn't demurely drink from the cup, but consumed the liquid in one greedy gulp before turning and hurling the bejeweled goblet at the gilded cage hanging beside them.

"Unfaithful bastard!"

Alarmed, the bird screeched, flapping its clipped wings and attempting to take flight. It was no use, of course, and Echo's heart pounded in her ears when she realized the bird had been caged as a repentance for Zeus's infidelities.

Echo scrambled to her feet. "I'm sorry to have offended you, my lady!"

Hera's gaze cut to her. The goddess said nothing, but the flare of her nostrils and the heave of her chest confirmed that her greatest insecurity had been dredged to the surface.

"Let me... tell you another story... a happier one..." said Echo, the lump in her throat making it difficult to get the words out.

"I'm tired of stories," replied Hera. She looked Echo directly in the eyes. "But, thanks to you, I am exceedingly curious what my husband is currently up to." With that, she strode out of her sanctuary, the willow branches parting obediently with a flick of her hand.

Tears sprang to Echo's eyes. Not only had she raised Hera's suspicion, something which

she had not meant to do, but she had also put
her sisters in terrible danger.

CHAPTER 8

ECHO RAN FROM Hera's sanctuary with tear-swollen eyes. She could not stop the goddess from searching for her wayward husband, but she could warn her sisters. She willed her legs to move faster as she ran out of the garden, ignoring Aphrodite, who gave her a quizzical look as she flew past. Instead of slowing, she pumped her arms harder, hoping against all hope they would propel her forward at the speed of light.

They did not, for she was only a nymph, possessing no power to winnow herself here or there like the goddesses did. It would take time to reach her sisters. Her only comfort was, for all Hera knew, there were countless places Zeus could be, and an endless number of other women he could be seducing. Echo may not have the advantage of speed, but she did know the exact spot where she had seen Zeus and her sisters last.

Echo paid no mind to the jagged edges of tiny rocks hidden under the moldering leaves once she entered the forest. Sharp sticks cut her feet, yet she still moved with purpose, not slowing for anything. Her sisters' lives depended on it.

She skidded to a halt, however, when she heard a terrified scream. It was loud enough to be heard over the rushing water falling into the pool below.

"No," whispered Echo through her panting. "No, no, no, no."

She rushed over to the tree where she had spied the trio earlier and peered down on the scene.

Aethra, shivering as she tried to hide her nakedness. Hera standing before her, gaze fixed on a golden eagle circling high in the sky above them. A fish, gasping for air as it flopped on the pebbles next to Aethra's feet.

"You think I don't know all your tricks, husband?" screamed Hera. "Come down here and see what you have forced me to do!"

Aethra, seeing her chance to save Eudora while Hera was distracted, bent down to scoop up the flailing fish. Echo's hand flew to her mouth to stifle her own scream when Aethra whispered a farewell—or perhaps an apology—to the rainbow-scaled fish, kissed it quickly, and then ran to the pool and tossed it in. With a flash of a silver tail, the fish disappeared into the depths, their sister forever gone to them.

Hera snapped her head toward Aethra. "You think you saved her?" The enraged goddess's laugh was cruel as she stalked toward a now visibly shaking Aethra. "She will find her way to a stream soon enough, where she will be hunted and devoured by a ravenous predator."

Echo bit down hard on her knuckle, caught between staying silent to avoid notice and screaming at the top of her lungs to distract Hera.

Before she could decide, the goddess spoke.

"And now, since you are so eager to be tread upon, nymph." Hera pointed at Aethra, and with a downstroke of the goddess's finger, Aethra turned into a pile of pebbles, suspended in mid-air for the briefest of moments before dropping to the ground with the faint clatter of stone hitting stone.

The weight of the loss crashed down onto Echo. She had tried distraction and failed. Only now was it clear that she should have forbidden her sisters from meeting with Zeus, or perhaps asked Hestia or Demeter to speak with them, to dissuade them from their recklessness.

She'd failed not once, but twice.

The edges of her vision darkened, and she felt herself sinking to the forest floor, fainting despite the pain of the rough bark of the tree she'd been leaning on for support biting into her palms.

Echo had no idea how long she'd been out, only that her head ached and when her eyes blinked open, they found the silhouette of an eagle. Its cry pierced the air as it circled. Before she could sit up, a shadow fell over her.

"Did you really think you could play me for a fool?" asked Hera.

Echo sat upright, scrambling backward like a crab until her back hit the thin trunk of a sapling.

"Play you for a fool?" she repeated Hera's words. "No, I... just wanted to tell you a story."

Hera let out a bark of laughter. "You knew, nymph. Do not deny it. You will only make it worse for yourself."

Echo squeezed her eyes shut, believing Hera's threat wholeheartedly. She had just witnessed what the angry goddess had done to her sisters, and though she wished she had been able to save them, what was done was done. Echo did not want to end up with a similar fate.

"They had been seduced," said Echo, "and I only sought to give them time to..." Guilt wrapped its cruel tendrils around her throat, forcing her to suppress a sob instead of continuing.

"What?" spat Hera. "Fornicate with my husband?"

"No! To make the right choice, my lady."

"And you thought you could do this by using your gift of talk to deceive me?"

Echo had no choice but to nod. She was a storyteller, not a liar. There was no use denying the truth, which was she had tried to keep Hera on the mountain for a less than honorable reason. All that was left to do was wait for her judgment, and hope it was not death. Shame burned her cheeks as Hera looked her up and down, assessing how terrible a punishment she should inflict.

"Your gift will now be your curse," began Hera. "You shall speak no more unless someone has spoken first."

CHAPTER 9

Echo stared at the ground in confusion, heart still racing from her brush with death. The gods and goddesses spoke in riddles when casting their curses, and Hera had been no exception. But what did her words mean, exactly? Could Echo not tell stories unless someone asked? Lost in the thought, Echo shook her head. She couldn't fathom it.

The goddess sniffed haughtily as Echo reeled, her mind spinning off into a thousand directions. She would have to puzzle it out later, once this terrible encounter had come to an end. Right now, she must show the goddess she was grateful her life had been spared.

Echo kept her gaze lowered, waiting—hoping—the goddess was satisfied enough to walk away. But Hera was not finished.

"It seems you do not agree with the punishment I have handed down to you," said Hera.

Echo's head snapped up, her tear-filled gaze colliding with Hera's vicious glare.

"No, I was only trying to—"

"Silence!" commanded Hera, bending down to clamp a hand over Echo's mouth. "Your shameless pride and incessant talking have led you here, nymph, yet you continue to speak out of turn."

A whimper escaped Echo's throat when Hera tightened her merciless grip. The pain grew worse as she pulled Echo to her feet by her chin. She held in a cry of anguish, even though her jaw felt as though it might shatter.

"No more power will your voice have," said Hera. "No more grand stories will you tell. Your words will be yours no more. From now on, you will speak only when spoken to, repeating naught but the last words spoken to you." Finally, Hera released Echo with a violent push. "This is the justice I take for your trickery."

Hera's eyes flashed, a jagged stream of light shooting forth and connecting with Echo's throat. The pain was immense, burning like wildfire and leaving the taste of ash in her mouth.

"Trickery," rasped Echo, alarm immediately furrowing her brows, for that was not what she intended to say.

She had meant to beg Hera to reconsider, to let her keep her knack for storytelling, the only thing in which Echo took any pride, but it seemed Hera's curse was already at work.

"Yes, Echo," replied Hera. "The forfeit of your own words is the price you must pay for your deceit."

"Deceit... Deceit... Deceit!" cried Echo as the goddess turned on her heel and walked away.

Distraught at the loss of her ability to speak freely and at will, for she had tried to no avail, Echo had collapsed into a sobbing heap onto the forest floor. Clouds rolled by, birds sang, woodland creatures came to sniff at her, but she had lain there, with her knees curled to her chest, for three days.

On the morning of the fourth day, a fierce growling startled her awake. Her stomach tightened in fear. Only when a painful rumble seized her insides did she realize the menacing sound had come from her.

Slowly, Echo pushed herself up to sitting and looked around. She frowned at the way the breeze still blew, how the sun still rose and set, how life went on while she grappled with the loss of something that had given her purpose. She sighed. Despite her grief, time had not stopped to wait. It had not slowed but carried on without her.

She rose to her feet, which were covered in dirt. She would go to the stream, not only to cleanse her body, but to wash away her sadness. After that, she would fill her empty stomach with berries. Perhaps gathering a handful of wildflowers might also lift her spirit. She would revel in the sweet scents of sage, lupine, primrose... lilies.

She decided against picking flowers as she made her way to the stream. Though she was beginning to accept her new circumstance, her head and heart were still aching and raw. She wasn't ready to see or smell or touch anything associated with Hera.

Echo knelt, peering at the reflection staring up at her from the water's glassy surface. She frowned at the sticks and moss embedded in her hair, and her dirty face, still bearing evidence of how many tears she'd shed. She looked a fright, but it was fitting. She felt like one, too.

She dipped her hands into the water and brought it to her face, scrubbing until her cheeks were fresh and clean. Next, she sat on her heels and began to comb her fingers through her long tresses, which any passerby would surely think were the color of bark instead of cornsilk.

A faint pounding floated on the breeze. Echo stilled, cocking her head to listen. Hooves, and whatever animal was running for its life was heading straight for her. She whirled around, moving to a crouch and preparing to dart out of the way.

Heart racing as swiftly as the hooves, she scanned the woods. She saw nothing, only heard the hoofbeats getting closer and closer. And then, the bay of a hound in pursuit.

Hunters.

No sooner had she thought this, she spied a pair of antlers bouncing through the trees. As they rushed closer, she could see they belonged to a stag, leaping over fallen trunks as it ran for its life. She watched, transfixed, before quickly realizing she was directly in its path, and the stag didn't see her, only its escape.

Echo darted for safety behind a fallen tree, narrowly avoiding being trampled. She held her breath when the magnificent animal leapt over the stream, an arrow hanging from its flank, bobbing up and down before falling out from the force of its landing. Echo winced. The barb had taken some of the animal's flesh with it. It was not a mortal wound, and the stag would live to see another day.

That was, if the hound was distracted from its chase.

Her gaze snapped to the direction from which the stag had come, and, as if on cue, the hound appeared. Its nose was to the ground, only lifting it to unleash a howling bark; a signal indicating to the hunter it still followed the scent of their prize.

Without thinking, Echo mimicked the hound, cupping her hands around her mouth to amplify the sound.

Ah-wooh, ah-wooh, ah-wooh!

She peeked over the top of the moss-covered trunk, ignoring the strong smell of dirt and rot. The hound skidded to a halt, tilting its head and cocking its ears. It whined in confusion as it paced back and forth, vexed at the presence of another hound.

CHAPTER 10

ECHO DUCKED DOWN when she heard the crunch of footsteps, hurried but not running. By the sound of it, only one hunter approached, but that did not mean there weren't more on the way.

Echo bit her lip, unsure of what to do next. Why had she felt the need to save the stag, especially after failing her sisters and ending up cursed? She dug her hands into the soft earth, rubbing it over the bare skin of her arms to disguise her scent. If the hound caught wind of her, she would be doomed.

The hound whined again before unleashing another *Ah-wooh!*

"It's okay, boy." The hunter's voice was like a song, the timbre smooth and sweet, and it caused Echo to immediately abandon her task. She dropped the moss she had been putting in her hair and, moving as quietly as a mouse, peeked over the top of her hiding place to get a look at the man whose voice was as soothing as a lullaby.

She nearly gasped when she saw him. True, she hadn't seen many mortals, but he was the most beautiful man she had ever laid eyes upon. His handsome face was smooth, his jaw strong and free of hair. Her gaze moved down to his broad chest before going back up to his glossy dark hair, unable to keep herself from staring at the way it caressed his temples and eyelashes.

He splashed through the stream, and Echo's heart skipped a beat when he crouched down to pick up the arrow.

"It was no good anyway," he mumbled, turning it over in his hands, examining it for defects as the hound lay beside him, waiting for its next command with a thumping tail.

The young man sighed before standing. He was tall and lean, with finely shaped arms and calves. A warmth ignited low in Echo's belly, flaring to life in her a strange ache that made her wonder how his long fingers would feel as they brushed over her skin, and if his lips would feel soft pressed against hers...

"Come on, then," he said, reaching down to scratch behind the hound's ears. "Let's find the others."

Echo watched as the hunter and his hound headed off into the direction from which they had come. An odd panic surged through her. Who knew how long she'd be forced to wander these woods alone, unable to speak unless spoken too? What if she never saw anyone again?

What if she never saw *him* again?

On impulse, Echo snatched up a nearby stone and tossed it into the stream. It bounced off a larger rock and landed on the wet pebbles with a splash.

When Echo gathered enough courage to look, she saw the hunter had turned around to scan the area, and she had a moment of regret when the hound unleashed a menacing growl. She'd overheard other nymphs tell of how they could effortlessly blend in with their surroundings in times of danger simply by willing it so. She hoped the rumor was true— she had never had such a need—but in case it wasn't, she dropped to all fours and climbed inside the trunk through a small opening. In case it wasn't, she dropped to all fours and climbed inside the trunk through a small opening. Though the jagged bark scraped at her narrow shoulders and hips, she thanked the goddesses it was just big enough for her to fit. Curled into a ball, she prayed what little moss she did manage to apply to her hair would be enough to camouflage her should he come investigate.

"Who's there?" he called out, his approaching footsteps slow and careful.

A crow cawed, another answering in the distance. Echo closed her eyes and clenched her teeth, the urge to repeat his words nearly unbearable. She bit down so hard, concentrating on remaining quiet, the sound of two more sets of footsteps barely registered.

It wasn't until she heard a second voice, then a third, that she realized the hunter was no longer alone. The others had caught up with him.

"Talking to yourself again, Narcissus?" came a second voice. The man's footsteps were heavy, indicating he was much larger in size.

His voice was deeper, too, and much less soothing to Echo's ears. But the younger man, the one with the beautiful face and pleasing build...

Narcissus, she thought to herself, *what a fine name.*

"And this surprises you, father?" said the third voice, a boy who scattered Echo's thoughts with his braying laughter.

"I see the stag has escaped," said the father, ignoring the boy to deliver a taunt of his own. "I suppose you're going to tell me it's the arrow that's at fault and not the hunter's skill."

"That's exactly what I will tell you, father, because it's true," said Narcissus. "The fletching was too long for a straight shot."

Echo lifted her chin from her chest and craned her ear. Narcissus was exasperated, and the mere sound of his distress made her chest tighten.

"Well, if you spent more time learning how to make your own arrows and less time talking to yourself in the woods, you'd be better at earning your keep," said the boy with a nasally whine.

"Oh, would you shut up, Keos," said Narcissus.

Echo found herself offended on Narcissus's behalf. *Yes, shut up, Keos.*

"Stop bickering, you two," said their father. "We'll try again tomorrow."

Echo strained to listen as two sets of footsteps, one heavy, one light, receded into the forest, until a loud snuffling next to her head drowned them out. When she realized what was making the noise, she nearly bleated out in fear.

Go away! She silently commanded the nosey beast, but it was no use.

"What is it, boy?" said Narcissus.

Echo's heart pounded in her ears as she looked up through a small hole in the bark. All she saw was a sliver of blue sky, but she knew he was so close that he could surely hear the way her heart hammered. She squeezed her eyes shut, pulling her arms tighter against her chest while trying to steady her breathing.

The hound whined.

Please don't see me, please don't see me, please don't...

The sliver of bright sky went dark, causing Echo's eyes to pop open against their will.

Narcissus flinched, gasping when their eyes met, but immediately bent closer to investigate.

"Who are you?" he whispered.

Echo swallowed hard before answering. "You?"

Narcissus's eyes went wide at the same time his mouth dropped open. It looked as though he were about to speak, but a sharp whistle sounded off in the distance, causing his gaze to snap upward. After a moment, he set his lovely dark eyes on her once more before drawing backward and vanishing from view.

Echo felt the trunk shake when he hopped onto it, then heard the light thump when he landed on the other side. She listened to the

soft patter of his feet as he ran away, leaving
her desperately trying to remember how to
breathe.

CHAPTER 11

ECHO HAD RUN from her hiding place straight to Olympus without stopping. Finally, she slowed to a walk, panting as she entered the garden. The encounter with Narcissus had left her dazed, confused, and most strangely of all, longing with every fiber of her being to see him again. She knew he would search the forest for her now that he had seen her, the look on his face had said as much.

Was there such a thing as love at first sight?

It seemed there was, and Echo would ask Aphrodite how one should proceed having been struck by one of her son's arrows. Who would know better about these things than the goddess of love herself? Besides, as powerful as she was, perhaps Aphrodite could lift Hera's curse.

Echo prayed she wouldn't see the queen of the gods as she stepped onto the expansive stone veranda where they would sit while she told—used to tell—her stories. If her prayers went unanswered and she did see the woman who had done this to her, she hoped she at least didn't appear like a panting and disheveled mess.

She slowed her breathing even further as she made her way toward the rose garden, the place where Aphrodite liked to spend her time while on Olympus. Echo's stomach looped as she approached. If Aphrodite wasn't here, it meant she was with a lover, and Echo certainly wasn't going to interrupt.

Echo sighed with relief when she smelled the scent of roses on the breeze and hurried under the arched trellis laden with fragrant blooms.

"My sweet mountain child, where have you been?" asked Aphrodite, alarm etched across her face as she pushed up from her cushioned reclining couch when she spied Echo. "And what on Earth has happened?"

It was then Echo realized that she hadn't bathed in the stream like she had intended. In fact, she had added more dirt to her person, and for nothing, since it hadn't disguised her at all.

The thought brought her back to earlier events, to the look of confusion on Narcissus's face, and then irritation when she had tried to speak to him. It had stirred in her a feeling she could not describe. His reaction made her longing to be near him even stronger than when she'd first seen him, with an urge to run after him when he left so intense it frightened her. The chance meeting had spurred in her something she could not control, let alone grasp the meaning of, and she needed to know how to reconcile these feelings with the bliss she also felt. They vacillated with one another, first hope and joy, then confusion and despair.

But how would Echo explain all this without being able to speak until spoken to first?

"Happened. Happened. Happened," she repeated, nodding vigorously.

Aphrodite tilted her head, and though she furrowed her brow deeply, no lines marred her perfect face. "What has gotten into you, dear one?"

"Dear one!" said Echo, pointing down at the ground and then tapping her heart with her fingers. "Dear one."

"I say, stop these riddles and use your words."

Echo unleashed an exasperated huff and did indeed stop trying to explain. But a tiny smile curled her lips when the sounds from the nearby pond drifting on the breeze gave her an idea. She pointed at the willow off in the distance.

"Words," she said before placing her other hand over her mouth.

That seemed to have done the trick, for Aphrodite arched both brows. "Have you been cursed?"

"Cursed!" cried Echo, her eyes going wide as she nodded. "Cursed! Cursed!"

Echo tapped two fingers high on her cheek, just below her eye, before pointing at the ground again. When she clasped her hands over her breast, Aphrodite's face smoothed with understanding.

"Oh, dear," she sighed. "Cursed by Hera no less, and probably something to do with Zeus," Aphrodite rolled her eyes. "But you've fallen in love with a mortal, down on Earth, is that it?"

Echo's smile was sad, her nod slight. That was indeed her current plight.

Aphrodite placed a hand on Echo's shoulder. Though she did so lightly, it felt as though an anchor weighted Echo down, crushing the last of her spirit the curse had not already taken.

"Hera is my queen," said Aphrodite. Her tone was solemn, but her aquamarine eyes were full of pity as she picked a clump of moss out of Echo's hair. "I can see in your eyes you are hoping I can break the curse, but I'm afraid

I cannot undo what has not been done by my hand, dear one." She tucked an errant lock behind Echo's ear. "But I can help you feel better. Come."

Echo did not protest when Aphrodite slipped an arm around her shoulders and led her out of the garden and into a small grotto a short distance away. Nor did she say a word when, with a wave of the goddess's hand, rose petals floated on the surface of the hot spring inside.

"A long soak will do you good," said Aphrodite, gesturing toward the steaming water.

The goddess looked at her pointedly, and Echo knew there was another meaning tied up within the words, one she didn't have the will to untangle. She simply nodded and smiled sweetly, sending Aphrodite the false notion that she would bathe as the goddess had suggested.

Aphrodite smiled. It was so bright and dazzling, it made Echo feel even worse for what she was about to do.

"Wonderful," said Aphrodite. "Come see me when you are finished, won't you? If you cannot tell me a story, I shall try my best to entertain you with one of mine."

Echo appreciated Aphrodite's kindness—it wasn't often a goddess cared so much about a nymph—but she was too heartbroken and lovesick to accept it. All she wanted was to go back to her forest, so she could search for Narcissus. She must see him again, even if it took an eternity.

She pretended to unwrap her dress, taking a few steps toward the hot spring for good measure. When the grotto fell silent, Echo glanced over her shoulder to make sure the goddess was gone. When she saw that she was alone, she quickly pulled her dress up over her shoulder and turned around.

"Mine, mine, mine..." whispered Echo, walking out of the grotto before breaking into a run.

CHAPTER 12

ECHO PEERED THROUGH the crack in the wood. When a twig snapped loudly underfoot, she froze in place. Narcissus, who had come without his canine companion this time, whirled around to face the tree she was hiding behind. Echo held her breath. She had been following him for weeks, watching him and longing to make herself known, but not knowing what to do if she did.

Of course, the Fates would choose this moment to grow impatient with her silent stalking.

"I saw you in the fallen tree that day," called out Narcissus, abandoning his usual demands to know who was spying on him. When she did not answer, he continued. "I know you follow me. Why do you think I've come back so many times?"

Heart hammering, Echo bit her lip at the thought he longed to know her as much as she did him. If this were true, why did a pit form in her stomach when she thought of showing herself to him?

"Very well," said Narcissus, moving to make himself comfortable at the edge of the stream. "Since you refuse to tell me who you are, then I shall tell you who *I* am." He sat with his arms resting on his knees. "Though I suppose you already know, I am Narcissus, son of Endymion, and the best hunter in my village."

Echo could not stop herself from giggling at the embellishment, ducking behind the tree just in time for his narrow-eyed gaze to miss her.

"Fine," he exhaled. "Second best, but only to father. I have a..." He hesitated, but only for a heartbeat. "Brother. One who thinks he's better than me. He's not, though."

His chin lifted ever so slightly, as if daring her to disagree. The gesture was defiant, but there was something else in the way he arched his brow that gave it less certainty and more of a longing for reassurance. Echo found herself wanting to put her arms around his neck, to stroke his dark hair as she whispered into his ear.

There was no one like him. No one who could even compare.

"My mother is the moon goddess, you know," he said, breaking Echo's reverie. "Selene. The one who glows bright in the night sky. I've never seen her in mortal form, only when she is the moon. I am told we have her eyes." A sardonic laugh escaped him. "And her alluring presence. Apparently, that's why so many people want to be close to us..."

His words trailed off but, lost in her own thoughts, Echo didn't notice how he spoke as if the moon was also *her* mother, or that he had been on the verge of saying more.

She had no doubt he was the son of Selene. He was beautiful to behold, with a magnetism that could not be resisted. She lowered herself to the ground, quietly turning around and resting her back against the trunk. She could not deny it was curious the way Narcissus spoke of himself as though he were another person. It seemed he had a story to tell, and she knew how long stories could take, they could be there for hours, but she would sit and listen for as long as he spoke.

When she realized he had gone silent, she peeked around the trunk, holding her breath and waiting for him to continue.

"I had a sister once, a twin." Narcissus was barely audible. "But she died."

Echo's breath caught.

"I miss her," he said, scooting toward the edge of the bank. "Sometimes, when I can't remember what she looked like, I do this..." He leaned over and peered into the water. "And it's like you're still here."

Echo watched with wide eyes as Narcissus stared at his reflection. "It wasn't my fault," he murmured. "I didn't mean to..."

A tear slid down the bridge of his perfect nose, but he wiped it away before it could drop and moved away from the water's edge.

Echo's heart ached, and she almost went to him, but he resumed relaying the ease of his childhood and bolstering his accomplishments, and so she stayed put. She would admit, it felt strange not to be the one telling the story, but she quite liked the sound of his voice. She was happy the sadness was gone from it, so she listened to every word, absently weaving a crown out of nearby twigs, long twine, and sprigs of brush with glossy leaves.

He talked until the sun went down and the crickets chirped, a great horned owl occasionally interrupting their song. She'd finished the crown and was admiring her handiwork under the moonlight when she heard Narcissus stir.

"I must go now," he said.

Chirp.

"Are you still there?"

Chirp, chirp.

"I grow tired of this," he said, frustration at going weeks without a response evident by his harsh tone. "If you wish for me to come back, you must answer me aloud."

Even though it seemed like time was standing still, Echo was suddenly on her feet. If she did not answer, this might be the last time she would see Narcissus. Rough bark bit into her palms as she gripped the tree, staring at Narcissus and opening her mouth to speak.

Before she could say anything, Narcissus made one last demand, raking his hand through his hair as he did so. "Do you want me to come again?"

"Again, again, again!" shouted Echo.

"Very well," said Narcissus, satisfied at finally having gotten an answer. "Then I shall see you again tomorrow."

Echo placed a hand on her chest after he was gone, inhaling and exhaling slowly through her nose to further calm her breathing and guttering heart. If she wanted Narcissus to keep returning, she would have to show herself to him tomorrow.

The owl hooted, breaking the silence that had descended, and Echo bent down to pick up the crown she'd made. As she did, she spied a white flower glowing in the dim light a few feet from where she'd been sitting. She hadn't noticed it while she'd been fashioning the crown, but as she drew closer, Echo saw it was a moonflower.

She had thought the crown was merely something to keep her hands occupied while listening to Narcissus. She had planned to leave it for one of the satyrs to find, but seeing this clear message from Fate, perhaps even from Selene herself, she understood why—and for who—she'd been compelled to make it.

She plucked the flower and tucked it into the woven circlet as she made her way over to the stream.

"Tomorrow," she said, laying the crown in the very spot where the son of the moon goddess had last been.

CHAPTER 13

Six years later

THE SHARP SCENT of evergreens warmed by
the sun filled the air, and the golden morning
light filtered through the leaves, creating a
breathtaking scene before her. The picturesque
mountain setting of her home had always
brought Echo immense joy. Yet, nothing
compared to the beauty of the young man
walking through the trees toward the stream—
their stream—or the complete and utter thrill
of knowing he came to this place to be with her.

Echo's heart raced when his eyes widened
in delight when he spied the crown, her
shoulders dipping a moment later when he
pulled out the flower and tossed it aside. He
must not know it had closed with the arrival of
dawn but would reopen once twilight
descended, thinking it wilted and spent
instead. Her sadness was soon forgotten,
however, when Narcissus placed the crown
atop his head, his lips curling into the barest
hint of a smile.

"Are you here?" said Narcissus.

"Here?" replied Echo.

"Yes, I am here," he replied. "And I see you've left me something." He puffed his chest and cocked his head. "How does it look?"

"Look," giggled Echo.

Narcissus frowned, standing with his hands on his hips as the water beside him trickled over the rocks. "How can I see my...? Ah, yes, of course." He knelt at the edge of the stream, leaning over so he could gaze at himself wearing his new crown. "It's a bit too small for my head, but I think it still suits me well."

Satisfied, he spread out on the bank, lying under the sun with his fingers linked behind his head. Echo inhaled deeply, anxiously waiting for him to say the right words so she could finally step out into the open.

"I've been wondering..." he began, "Why do you only repeat what *I* say? Why not speak for yourself?"

"Speak for yourself?"

"Yes, that is what I said," replied Narcissus, sitting up. "I grow tired of this game, you know."

"You know."

"I don't know!" he said, one hand flying up in frustration.

How quickly he became incensed, and oh, how badly Echo wanted to speak her own words. At the very least, the first instead of the last, but all that came out of her mouth was an equally irritated, "I don't know!"

Narcissus unleashed a heavy sigh, resigned to lead the conversation once more. He was silent for a moment or two, clearly contemplating a new thought. "You're not the *eidolon* of my sister, are you?"

"Are you?" said Echo, then immediately pressed her lips tight so she would not say anything more and upset him again.

She was cursed, but she most certainly was no spirit. She was alive and breathing and desperately in love. The only trouble was, she could not speak of her own free will to explain, let alone confess, and so she would wait for him to say the right words.

"I suppose I am," he sighed, surprising Echo with his resignation. "When people look at me, they see her. I think it's why my father treats me so poorly." Narcissus was quiet for a moment. "Prove to me I am not mad. Come to me."

Echo's heart nearly exploded in her chest. The Fates had been listening, finally compelling him to say the words she'd been longing to hear. Like a moth to a flame Echo stepped out of her hiding spot and rushed toward him with open arms.

"Come to me."

Narcissus shrank back in surprise the moment he saw her running for him.

"W-who are you?"

"W-who are you?" repeated Echo.

"I've told you, many times!" he shouted as he continued to scramble backwards. "I am Narcissus."

"I am Narcissus," Echo's response was as insistent as his.

Narcissus's smooth cheeks grew an angry red, his lips screwing into a furious sneer. "You mock me!"

"You mock me!" The words came out with the same venom, yet she did not abandon her advance. *"Ask me if I'm cursed!"* she screamed inside her head as she reached out and touched his shoulder.

"Don't touch me!" said Narcissus, shrugging her off.

Echo dropped her hand to her side, tears stinging her eyes. "Don't touch me!" she said, though the words *"I love you!"* echoed inside her head.

"I don't know who you are, girl, but you have wasted my time with your games," spat Narcissus. "I only returned here, time and time again, because I thought you were my sister, come back from beyond the grave to forgive me."

CHAPTER 14

THE WORDS LANDED like a blow, sending all the oxygen in Echo's lungs streaming out in a rush. She placed a hand on her chest, trying to pull in precious air as she staggered backwards. All this time he had thought she was the spirit of his dead sister.

The revelation he had not come for any other reason but forgiveness devastated Echo. He did not love her, he loved only his sister, enough to believe that she would come back from the Underworld to assuage his guilt.

For the first time since laying eyes on him, Echo's pulsed jumped with fear. What had he done?

When Echo was finally able to breathe, she whispered, "Forgive me."

Narcissus glared at her with fists and jaw clenched tight.

"Forgive me, forgive me, forgive me..." she pleaded.

She was mortified, stripped of the last thing that had given her hope that she could still be happy in this life, but when Narcissus turned to leave, she could not bear the thought of never seeing him again.

"Forgive me," she called after him.

"Stop it!" cried Narcissus, clasping his hands over his ears.

She tried not to repeat his last words, but it was no use. It burst forth like a waterfall, shooting from her mouth with brutal force. "Stop it!"

Narcissus spun around, eyes glassy and wild, and charged toward her with flared nostrils. "I've had enough of your nonsense, girl." He tore the crown from his head and threw it into the woods behind her. "Go back to wherever it is you came from and never speak to me again!"

Echo watched the crown sail over her head. She was taken by surprise when he shoved her. The breath left her lungs, and time moved in slow motion in the seconds before Echo hit the ground, a horrified gasp filling the air just before the world went dark.

"I'm sorry."

His voice sounded far away, as though she was far below in the Underworld, and he was still miles above the earth. Determined to wade through the darkness toward him, Echo blinked her eyes open. When the world came back into focus, she was relieved to see Narcissus standing over her.

"I didn't mean to..."

His face was pinched with torment, his voice full of regret. She believed that he hadn't meant to harm her, but when he reached out to help her up, her instincts took over and she rolled away, unable to stop a frightened whimper from escaping her lips.

This was what had happened to his sister. He had struck her, out of anger or fear or jealousy, Echo could not say, but it had been hard enough to end her life.

Echo sprang to her feet, digging her toes into the earth for leverage as she sprinted away. Her heart tore in two as she ran, half wanting to keep going and never stop, the other half wanting to turn around and go back, to comfort the tortured boy she loved, easing his pain and soothing his suffering forever.

In the end, her body chose flight. He needed time alone and she needed time to think, and so she would hide among the trees until they both had calmed down.

Despite her logical mind, her breaking heart compelled her to turn her head and look back at him as she dashed farther into the trees. She sorely regretted it when, without warning, she collided with something soft but unyielding and went tumbling to the ground.

Overwhelmed and dazed, she rubbed her temples, wondering how many bruises she would have after this day, when a hand clasped onto her wrist.

"I've been searching for you, dear one," said Aphrodite.

Echo looked up at the goddess, who was staring down at her serenely, the ends of her ruby gold hair billowing in the same light breeze that rustled the leaves.

"You left Olympus so suddenly, without having set foot in the bath I had prepared for you," continued Aphrodite as she helped Echo to her feet. "Silly girl, the water was magical. It would have made you irresistible to anyone who gazed upon you." She stopped suddenly, her eyes flicking toward the direction Echo had come. "Who were you running from?"

Echo shook her head, shrugging lightly and hoping her nonchalance would convince Aphrodite without words that she was simply enjoying a good romp through the forest.

It seemed her casual shrug worked, for Aphrodite arched a brow and smiled.

"Have you become lovers with your mortal yet?" she asked. "Is he chasing after you?"

Echo sighed before dropping her gaze to her feet and shaking her head.

"No?" Aphrodite cupped Echo's chin, lifting her gaze to meet hers. Unable to tell her the true reason, Echo could do nothing but push her lips into a faint smile. Aphrodite released Echo's face to place a hand on her shoulder. "Well, we shall fix that. Lead me to him."

Hope fluttered in Echo's chest as she took Aphrodite's proffered hand, tamping down the shame that was trying to rise from the pit of her stomach and stop her legs from moving forward. She wasn't lying, they *weren't* lovers, but perhaps with Aphrodite's help, they still could be.

Echo walked ahead of the goddess a few paces, her thoughts warring inside her head as she led the way. *He is too consumed by his guilt to want you... His heart is closed because he is terrified to lose again... But if Aphrodite wants to enchant him into loving me back, who am I to keep a goddess from doing her will?*

She stopped at the edge of the clearing and waited for Aphrodite to catch up to her. Together, they watched Narcissus sit by the stream, the profile of his aquiline nose and full lips a study of perfection.

"What a beautiful young man," said Aphrodite. "I can see why you pine for him."

As if he heard, he turned his back to them, burying his head in his folded arms that rested on his knees.

"Go to him, dear one," said Aphrodite.

Echo doubted her presence so soon after being sent away would be received well, but she did as she was instructed and walked toward Narcissus until she stood in front of him.

"I told you to go away," said Narcissus without looking up, his voice muffled and thick with emotion. "I wish to be alone."

Echo lowered her head, tears springing to her eyes unbidden. She turned to look at Aphrodite, but the goddess had vanished.

"I call upon the divine power vested in me..." said Aphrodite, now standing behind Narcissus. Echo watched with bated breath as the goddess raised her arm, a great golden bow appearing in her hand as she did so. The instrument hummed loudly, glowing brightly as she leveled an arrow at his back. "To ensure this mortal will fall in love with the first face he sees."

The goddess of love let loose her arrow, and though it sunk deep into his back, Narcissus did not flinch. After a few moments of utter stillness, Aphrodite knelt beside him and placed a hand on his shoulder. When Narcissus still did not lift his head, Echo realized that he was too fraught with emotion to feel the presence of love, and only Echo could see and hear the goddess.

Echo looked at Aphrodite with a furrowed brow, asking the question with her eyes. *Did it work?*

"Be patient, dear one," she replied, already beginning to vanish, her good work having been done. "Love takes time." She gestured toward a clump of reeds along the opposite bank. "Wait for him nearby. The first face he lays eyes upon must be yours."

CHAPTER 15

NOT WANTING TO waste a gift from Aphrodite for a second time, Echo left Narcissus to his sorrow and settled among the tall reeds to wait.

The first face he lays eyes upon must be yours.

Aphrodite's words had been no riddle. This time, the goddess had been clear about what Echo was to do. She should watch over Narcissus with a hawk's eye and be ready to step into his line of vision at a moment's notice.

And so that is what she would do.

The birds sang as Helios traveled across the sky, but Narcissus did not look up. The sun glowed orange as it hung low on the horizon, still Narcissus did not look up. Though he no longer wept, he sat motionless for so long Echo wondered if he had turned to stone. Finally, when twilight blanketed the sky, he stirred. Her muscles went taut, ready to spring into action, but once she saw his movement was only to stretch out his long limbs and lay down, she relaxed.

A warm and gentle breeze blew the tops of the reeds, emitting a sound that made Echo's own lids grow heavy. The crickets chirped as the hazy purple of twilight ushered in the deep indigo of night. The moon was full, its light glinting off the stream and illuminating Narcissus's sleeping form.

Echo thought of creeping from her hiding place and lying next to him, so that when he awoke, she'd be the first person he would see. But the thought of him pushing her away, so unsettled and upset the last time she had shown herself to him, played over and over in her mind.

No, she would not resort to trickery. She would heed Aphrodite's words. *Be patient, dear one.* She would wait, and come out when the time was right, approaching him again when his heart was open, free from the pain and sorrow of his guilt.

And so, she settled in to sleep, secure in the notion that, come sunrise, he would see how she had remained by his side throughout his ordeal, despite his command for her to leave.

Echo's eyes fluttered open, the morning light warm on her face as her first and only thought entered her mind.

Narcissus.

The sound of water tumbling over rocks filled the air as she pictured his face, perfect even when...

Narcissus!

She bolted upright and pushed the reeds aside, praying to find him still asleep. The bright morning sun forced her eyes into a squint, but her blinking and watery gaze still managed to find Narcissus.

Her mouth dropped open when she saw him leaning forward to drink from the stream. She admired the way his muscles moved beneath his smooth skin as he dipped a cupped hand into the water. When he stopped abruptly, leaning closer and staring in wide-eyed wonder, as though he saw something so lovely, her brows angled. Something had clearly caught his eye, but what?

And then her heart nearly stopped, the words Aphrodite had said to her, that hers must be the first face he sees, ringing inside her head.

She jumped up and ran toward him, trying to tell him not to look at his reflection, but all that would come out was a strangled cry. She waved her hands at him as she drew near, trying to draw his attention away from the glassy surface of the stream.

But it was too late. Narcissus stared at his reflection; his eyes soft with love for the face looking back at him with the same smitten longing.

Echo splashed through the stream toward Narcissus, but he took little notice of her. If he did, he did not care, not until the rippling water made his reflection disappear.

His head snapped up, his gaze fixing on hers as she stood over him.

"You scared him away," he said, his voice laced with a mix of panic and irritation.

Narcissus leaned back, too preoccupied with the boy in the water to ask who she was or where she had come from. Echo sank to her knees, wishing she was small enough for the shallow water to carry her away, for he had looked directly at her and felt nothing.

"I hope he comes back," he said. "I should like to get to know him. He seems very interesting." Narcissus's cheeks reddened. "And the way he smiled at me... I think he feels the same. Do you know who he is?"

Echo shook her head, sadness pushing both her shoulders and her head down.

"Can I tell you a secret?" whispered Narcissus.

She looked at him, her heart breaking in two as she nodded.

"I felt something I've never felt before," he said. "A knowing deep in my heart. Out of all the people who wish to be close to me, this stunning creature, whoever he is, may be the only one who can truly see me."

Unable to control her emotion, Echo hiccupped. Pressure built behind her eyes, burning from holding back a torrent of tears on the verge of spilling. She'd waited so patiently, resisting the urge to ensure she would be the first person he saw when he awoke. How could the Fates have been so cruel? Her intentions had always been pure, she had always thought of others first, yet she was being punished for her kindness. She had nothing to show for her good deeds, for now she was here, in this awful moment, desperately in love with someone who loved only himself.

Anger and resentment suddenly took hold of her. Quick as lightning, she took his face in her hands and wrenched his gaze to meet hers.

"See me!" She cried. "See me, see me, see me!"

Narcissus did not recoil, nor did he push her away. He simply answered with a question.

"Do you think he'll come back?"

CHAPTER 16

NARCISSUS SAID NOTHING more. Even as Echo's hands slid from his face, his eyes stared through her vacantly, his mind somewhere else entirely. Her tears broke free, and she fell forward, laying her head on his chest and weeping. Her pent-up emotion drained out of her, and still, he did not move a muscle.

When he did speak, it was too soon.

"You must go now." Narcissus gently pushed Echo off his chest. "So that he will come back."

Echo's grief was made worse by the tender way he spoke, as though he did not want to offend her. Or perhaps it was his eagerness to see his reflection again. Either way, it was a far cry from how harshly he had treated her only hours ago.

When Narcissus gave the gurgling stream a sidelong glance, something foreign rose within Echo, causing her to wipe away her tears as she made a silent vow.

I will stay here with you forever, even after my broken heart stops beating. Wherever you go, I will follow. Whenever you call, I will answer.

Bone tired, Echo got to her feet. One way or another, she would break through to him. He was all she had left, and she would hold on to him for an eternity.

She smiled down at Narcissus. He returned her smile, but it was thin and forced. She ignored the sting of rejection when he trapped his bottom lip between his teeth, impatient for her to leave. With nothing else to do and nothing more she could say, Echo turned and walked toward the tree line. But like she'd done with Aphrodite, when she was sure his gaze had left her, she ducked behind a large clump of mountain sagebrush.

He sat there until sunset, gazing at himself in the water. Struck by Aphrodite's powerful arrow, he was enamored with his own reflection, and there was nothing Echo could do to get his attention. She had sent flowers downstream. She had tossed pebbles in his direction. She had even retrieved the crown he'd thrown away and laid it next to him while he slept.

The next morning, Narcissus crawled over to the edge of the stream without even noticing the crown. He looked down and smiled, remaining oblivious to everything around him but the young man in the water.

The hours turned into days, yet Narcissus did not leave the stream. If the day was cloudy, he would sigh as he waited for his love to appear. Despite her sorrow, Echo wished for the sun to come out. It was on sunny days when Narcissus smiled the brightest, and it gave her a burst of desperately needed happiness to see it.

But her joy was fleeting. To witness him conversing with his reflection as though another living being was truly there brought her great suffering. It pained her to hear him laughing at his own cleverness and blush when he complimented himself on his lovely dark eyes.

His body grew thin, and where there was once defined muscle, there was now shapeless skin clinging to bone. The dark half-moons under his eyes matched the shadows that had settled into his now hollow cheeks.

She wanted to go to him, but her mind had grown hazy, blanketed by a thick fog, yet strangely, her limbs felt heavier and lighter at the same time. It was difficult to move, and so she lay there, watching Narcissus fall more in love with himself.

It was worse than any torture she could have imagined, and after so many days of not being able to go to him and wrap her arms around his neck, she slept.

Echo's eyes fluttered open when she felt someone stroking her hair. Her heart raced, surprising her that it was even still beating. Had Narcissus finally grown tired of whispering sweet nothings to his reflection? She sat up, eager to look into his beautiful eyes, but it was not Narcissus.

"Echo?" said the young woman. "Is that you?"

The woman's voice gurgled, though Echo did not find it unpleasant. Rather, it was a soothing and serene sound to her ears. Her skin was mottled, like river rock, and her silt-colored hair was dripping wet. A water nymph, Echo guessed, one who had ventured onto dry land for a better look at the fellow nymph who had been lying motionless on the ground for days.

Concerned brows angled over the river nymph's gray eyes as she waited for an answer, but all Echo could do was blink as she thought about how to respond. She could not answer directly, only repeat the woman's last word, which would no doubt confuse her.

Echo nodded.

"Why do you lay here?" said the river nymph. "And who is that man who keeps looking at himself in the water, as though he is cursed—"

Echo's mind was awake in an instant, the fog evaporating upon hearing that one word. "Cursed!" She bobbed her head up and down as she sat up and pointed to her chest. "Cursed," she said, now pointing at Narcissus. "Cursed."

The river nymph's hand went to her mouth, her gray eyes widening. After her initial shock had faded, her hand fell away slowly.

"It's true, then," she said. "We heard a rumor Hera had cursed you, but we thought it only hearsay, for why would she curse *you*, the one who brings such joy to all?" The river nymph laid a hand on Echo's shoulder. "Oh, Echo, I'm so sorry."

Echo appreciated the comfort. Without thinking, she placed a hand over the river nymph's and took a deep breath.

"Sorry," she agreed, sighing heavily.

The river nymph's gaze cut to Narcissus. "What about him? Did Hera curse this man as well?"

Echo shook her head.

"Who, then?" asked the river nymph. "And why do you remain by his side?"

How in the world was she going to explain what had happened? Echo ran her tongue over her dry lips before pressing them together in determination. She must at least try.

She ticked her head toward Narcissus then placed a hand over her heart.

Tears welled in the river nymph's eyes. "Because you love him."

Echo closed her eyes and nodded, her own tears escaping to roll down her cheeks. She opened them so she could look into the woman's eyes as she pretended to pull back the string of a bow.

The river nymph gasped. "Artemis cursed him?"

Echo shook her head. It made sense the river nymph would think the perpetrator was the virgin goddess of the hunt. Artemis often warned nymphs about the perils of men, both mortal and divine.

The river nymph screwed up her mouth as she thought about what other divinity favored a bow and arrow. Echo patted her heart, to help the woman come to the right conclusion. There was no way to explain to her that Narcissus had not been cursed, but enchanted.

"Eros?" replied the river nymph, tilting her head.

Echo's eyes went wide. The woman was so close.

"But I have never heard of the god of love cursing anyone except for..."

The woman bit the inside of her cheek, thinking. Echo's heart hammered in anticipation. She wasn't sure what the river nymph could do for either Narcissus or herself if she guessed correctly, but it felt good to be in the company of another, especially when the woman reminded Echo of her sisters.

The woman's face suddenly lit up. "Oh, I know!"

Echo's eyebrows shot up, ready to confirm the answer.

"Apollo!" cried the river nymph.

CHAPTER 17

ECHO PUT A finger to her lips, signaling for the woman to lower her voice. She peeked around the woman's shoulder, exhaling when she saw her shouting had not caused upset. Not that she thought it would. Narcissus had scarcely noticed anything around him for days. He hadn't touched the berries she'd left, nor had he sipped from the stream once, too preoccupied with waiting to see his lover again.

Echo's head spun at the thought. Worry collided with fear, chasing away any feeling of comfort from the distraction the river nymph offered. It's seemed like a game now, guessing who and what had sealed both Narcissus's and Echo's fates, and she no longer wanted to play.

Lightheaded, Echo laid down. With her head resting on her outstretched arm, she went back to watching Narcissus.

"I'm sorry," said the river nymph. "I didn't mean to upset you."

Echo did not answer, for her lids grew as heavy as her heart. The woman's words faded, and the world around her dimmed. She didn't wish to be rude, but she was suddenly so cold, and all she wanted was for the river nymph to stop her persistence and go away.

It seemed her prayer had been answered when Echo finally sank into oblivion. That is until the woman's loud gasp pulled Echo back from the weightless dark. She opened her eyes to find the river nymph staring down at her with a horrified expression. Echo furrowed her brow, confused as to what the woman could possibly be carrying on about now.

"You were flesh and bone when I first came upon you," said the woman in a rush. "But now..."

Echo did not understand what the woman meant. Flesh and bone? Of course, she was flesh and bone. They were all flesh and bone. She struggled to sit up, to chastise the woman and tell her to leave once and for all, but it seemed the last of her strength had vanished, and she fell to the ground in an exhausted heap.

The river nymph began to weep, her mouth going slack with pity and her chest heaving with despair.

"But now... now... now?" whispered Echo.

"I can see right through you," the woman replied, wiping away her tears with the heel of her hand. "You are disappearing."

It must have been the shock that gave her the strength, or perhaps the desire to see for herself if the woman spoke truth, but Echo managed to lift a hand to her face.

Her stomach twisted in on itself. The woman had not been lying. She could see through her palm. She turned it over to inspect the back of her hand but it was the same.

She was fading away.

She dropped her arm, unable to bear looking at it one moment longer. She inhaled, filling her lungs with air so that she could scream, but the only thing she managed to unleash was a weak whimper. Darkness seeped into the edges of her vision like spilled ink, slowly spreading until it became a black void swallowing her whole.

CHAPTER 18

THE LAST THING Echo remembered was the round, sweet face of a curious water nymph hovering over her. The image wavered like a mirage behind her eyes, and Echo watched helplessly as the woman's expression went from playful to horrified.

In an instant, a cold dread stole the breath from her lungs, forcing her into consciousness once more. There was a sensation of swaying, and she wondered if her lifeless body was lying in the bottom of Charon's boat, on its way across the River Styx. But there was no sound of waves, only a rhythmic beat keeping time with the pulsing in her aching temples. Desperate to know if she had passed from the living world into the spirit realm, she opened her eyes, slowly, relieved to see twinkling stars dotting the night sky above and not a dark, swirling mist of doom.

After a moment of admiring the sparkling lights, it registered that the drumming sound she heard was hooves on hard-packed earth. Echo's gaze shifted, and the next thing that came into view was a crown atop a head of dark curls.

She wasn't floating, someone was carrying her.

Narcissus?

She went to wrap her arms around his neck, but she was too weak to move. He was so solid, and she so relieved, all she wanted to do was sink into his warmth. At last, they would be together. She willed herself to stay awake, to see where he was taking her, but the longer she kept her eyes open, the more she noticed something wasn't quite right. His ears, they were too long, folding over and pointing downward. Her gaze cut to the man's eyes. They were striking, but the wrong color. And his nose was too broad.

"Aye, you are awake," said the satyr with a toothy grin. "My wife Aix said the storyteller nymph needed Pan's help."

Her heart thumped in her chest with panic before returning to a steady pace. Pan was the god of the mountain wilds, known for his love and care of all creatures dwelling in his mountains, but especially nymphs. Although she was not in the arms of Narcissus, she was in good hands.

"Help," whispered Echo.

"She said you was cursed by the queen," replied Pan. "Poor nymph, you."

Echo nodded, wondering if he could see her tears against her translucent skin, for he had certainly seen that she was slowly disappearing. How had he even found her in the dimming evening light?

"I tripped over you," he replied, as if he had heard her thoughts. "Don't worry, Pan will bring you somewhere safe."

Echo sighed, relaxing in the knowledge that she would be brought back from the brink of death soon. Being a god himself, and not a powerless divinity like her, Echo assumed the satyr knew his brethren on Olympus well. He was on his way there now; she was sure of it. He would kneel before Hera, showing the queen the desperate state one of his cherished denizens of his domain was in and begging her to remove the curse.

After being restored, she would find Aphrodite, finally able to use her words to explain how she had failed so many, including herself. She would appeal for the goddess of love to strike another arrow into the heart of Narcissus. She would give up her voice again if she had to, so long as she and Narcissus could finally be together.

Her gaze absently wandered to the crown nestled around Pan's horns as she thought of what she would say first.

"Aye, it's a fine crown," he replied. "You made it, didn't you? For him, the mortal by the stream." He didn't wait for Echo to answer. "Pan didn't steal it." He shook his head. "No, he asked the mortal if he could have it, but he got no answer, so he took it." Pan shrugged his shoulders in a matter-of-fact way. "Besides, it doesn't look like your mortal will be around much longer." Echo stiffened, as did the goat god when he realized the harshness of his words when she began to cry anew. There was no taking the truth back once it had been told, so he simply sighed as he looked down at her with pity. "There, there. Everything will be alright. It is a shame to let such a beautiful thing go to waste."

He mumbled the last part to himself, not intending for Echo to hear, for it held a double meaning. But she had heard, and she crumpled in his arms, devolving into a heap of sniffling hiccups.

Pan said nothing more, leaving her to regain her composure in silence. After a few minutes more of climbing, he slowed to a stop.

"Here we are," he said, turning sideways as he entered a crack in the side of a mountain.

The sky full of shimmering stars disappeared, replaced by the light of a lone flame dancing in the darkness. The air around them grew colder, and Echo shivered. Curious, she turned her head ever so slightly. She spied a torch affixed to the rocky wall, lighting a narrow passageway. There were many ways to get to Olympus, this must be a shortcut known only to Pan.

Trembling with cold, she nestled into the warm, thick fur on his chest as he lifted the torch from its cradle and proceeded to make his way down the corridor. It was low and narrow, and he had to hunch over her to pass through.

Echo expected Pan to keep walking once he entered the cavernous space beyond, but he stilled. Her heart nearly beat through her chest when he went low on his haunches and gently placed her on the ground.

"Rest in peace, poor nymph," he said, taking the crown from his head and placing it atop hers. "Even when you are gone, your story will live on. Pan promises you this."

He stood, staring down at her with sadness in his eyes. Bewildered, Echo stared up at him, panic making her limbs tingle to life.

Why was he not taking her to Olympus? Did he think she would fade completely before he got there? Was this her funeral?

"Goodbye," he murmured.

There was a finality in his tone, and as he turned and walked away, something strange happened. For one determination-filled moment, Echo found the strength to become whole once more, with flesh and bone as real and solid as his. Using every ounce of her newfound power, she reached for him, repeating the last word he'd said to her.

"Goodbye, goodbye, goodbye, goodbye..."

She had meant to say it loudly, but her last chance at salvation came out barely above a whisper, with each word getting fainter and fainter until there was only silence.

Pan stopped in his tracks. When his head tilted, listening curiously, Echo thought she had done it; that she had communicated her will to live. He would turn around and scoop her up and take her to Olympus.

She dropped her arm when he resumed walking, then her head when it was clear he thought he'd only heard the echo of his own voice.

Disappointment and despair overcame her, and all the strength she'd managed to pull from deep within ebbed out of her. Echo sighed, returning to the ghost of a woman she'd become.

CHAPTER 19

"Narcissus!"

Echo bolted upright, the voice still ringing in her head. She couldn't tell if she had dreamed it, fallen victim to the trickery of a phantom sound haunting her mind during a fitful sleep, or if someone had entered the cave calling her love's name.

"Narcissus!" came the voice again, pitched tight with urgency. "Are you in here?"

Echo jumped to her feet this time, the hairs on her arms standing on end. It was real, not a dream, and whoever was looking for Narcissus was getting closer.

The voice sounded familiar—on the verge of manhood—but she still couldn't quite place it. Nor could she comprehend how she was suddenly standing, let alone rushing forward.

There was no time to understand it, she must reserve the energy she'd been granted to alert whoever had come to her presence. Curse be damned, she would show them exactly where Narcissus was, and together they would go to him.

"Are you in here... here... here?" she called out.

When she heard the voice that bounced off the cavern walls, she shuffled to a stop. Even though she was sure she had felt the muscles around her ribs and in her chest tighten as she'd pushed the words from her mouth, the voice that came out was not her own.

The boy called out again. "Narcissus!"

Echo bolted into action once more, running as swiftly as her legs would carry her through the passageway. "Narcissus, Narcissus, Narcissus!"

She blinked at the brightness as she emerged from the dark into the light. There, at the narrow mouth of the cave stood Keos, the brother of Narcissus. He looked so much younger now that he was alone. Before, when he had been secure his elder brother would always be around to taunt, he had seemed older than his years.

Echo recognized the guilt in the boy's eyes as he cupped both hands around his mouth. He thought his brother's disappearance was his fault. His jests had been too cruel, and his jabs had been too sharp, and his brother had left him to live with their world-weary and apathetic father alone.

"Narcissus!" the boy bellowed. "I'm sorry. Come back!"

Echo shook herself out of her stupor and began to move again. This moment was not the time to take inventory of the boy's appearance, or reasons for finding his brother. Now that the gods had given her the strength, she would use it to show herself to Keos. She would repeat every word he spoke, even if every single one of them that fell from her lips made no sense. It would not stop her from leading Keos to Narcissus, so together they could drag him away from the stream.

"I'm sorry! Come back... back... back!" said Echo as she rushed toward Keos, reaching out a hand.

Panic exploded in her body and confusion flooded her mind when the boy dropped his arms to his sides as his own voice echoed off the cavern walls before a deafening silence descended. Then, the boy looked right through her, as if she was not there at all.

Echo held her breath and braced for impact. An all-consuming terror seized her when she passed through him, stumbling to a stop on the other side of his solid form.

Stunned, she whirled around, reaching for Keos a second time. Her hand passed through him, swiping the air and causing her to almost lose her balance as he stood there, unable to see her.

All that he heard was the haunted sound of his own voice.

The boy began to cry. Overwhelmed and frightened of her new reality, Echo repeated his sobs. It was the only thing she could do, for all that remained now was her spirit. She could not be seen, nor touched, only heard, forever echoing the last words spoken to her, in a voice that was not hers.

A hound brayed in the distance, prompting Keos to hastily wipe away his tears. He sniffed once, swallowing down the rest of his emotion before exiting the cave to continue his search. Echo watched him go; unaware he had left her to stand alone in silence.

Her head was a cyclone, with a whirlwind of thoughts violently crashing into one another until there was only one left. She didn't know how or why, but it was clear the silent vow she'd made had become a self-fulfilling prophecy.

I will stay here with you forever, even after my broken heart stops beating. Wherever you go, I will follow. Whenever you call, I will answer.

Beholden to the promise she'd made, Echo fled the place where she had withered away; her feet never touching the ground as she flew toward the stream where Narcissus still lay. She would be with him until he took his last breath, and her love for him would live on, echoing through time forever.

CHAPTER 20

ECHO WAS SURPRISED to see Aphrodite at the stream. The goddess was kneeling, her long hair falling in perfect golden waves as she stroked an emaciated Narcissus's cheek. His eyes were closed, face gaunt, and the pallor of his skin was so dull and sickly, it made her want to look away. If it weren't for the shallow breaths belaboring his lungs, Echo would have thought him already gone.

Echo spread her arms wide, leaning forward and letting the wind carry her. As she drew closer, she saw the goddess's eyes brimming with glittering tears. The sight of it tightened her jaw with something she couldn't name.

Her feet touched ground once more, and when she fought the urge to push Aphrodite away from Narcissus, she realized it was anger, which was something she had rarely, if ever, felt before.

She felt raw and wild, desperate to gouge and bite, kick and scream. She had lost everything—her freedom, her voice, her life— and now the most cherished thing she had left was being taken. She could not mourn the passing of her true love alone. Not even the memory of his last moments would be hers to keep.

But she would never dare to show such petulance to a goddess.

"Oh, dear one," said Aphrodite, looking up. Her voice was filled with immense sorrow. "He saw his own reflection, didn't he?"

Echo's anger melted away. She nodded as she swallowed down the guilt trying to rise in her throat. This was not Aphrodite's fault. The goddess had tried to help her, more than once, but Echo had been foolish, too obsessed with pleasing others and doing what *they* wanted, what she thought was best for *them*, instead of staying true to her own heart. She should have done what she had wanted to do that first night, when Narcissus lay sleeping. Oh, how she wished she could turn back the hands of time.

Aphrodite stood. "I can't bear it," she said, taking both of Echo's hands in hers. "The ugliness of loving one's own self too much." She pulled Echo into her embrace. "He could have been so much more had he only seen you."

Echo wept. Yes, if he had only seen *her*, and not his reflection, he may have survived. Perhaps they both would have.

"It is time to say goodbye," murmured Aphrodite, releasing Echo.

She knelt beside Narcissus, wanting to shake him in one last attempt to bring him back. Instead, Echo pressed her lips to his. When she drew back, she saw him as he had been, not as he was then; wasted away and on the verge of death.

"Goodbye," said Echo, caressing his cheek.

His eyes fluttered open at her gentle touch, searching for whoever or whatever had brought him out of the darkness. When he finally fixed his gaze on her, it was frightened, for he knew this was the end.

"Will you tell him one last thing for me?"

Heart falling with the tears streaming down her face, she nodded, promising she would deliver his final message.

"Tell him..." whispered Narcissus. "I will always love you."

Echo's bottom lip trembled under the weight of those three words, so bittersweet to bear.

"I will always love you... love you... love you..." Echo whispered back.

With a wave of Aphrodite's compassionate hand, Narcissus disappeared before her very eyes. In his place grew a beautiful white bloom that resembled the moon flower, but with a ring of gold at its center.

A crown.

For this, Echo was grateful. Although it broke her heart he was gone, never to be seen again, the world could still gaze upon his beauty.

EPILOGUE

With nowhere else to go, Echo went back to the cave. It was there she stayed, listening to the fluttering of leathery wings and the scuttling of creatures seeking refuge day and night. She rarely ventured outside, but when she did, it was to admire the white flower with its golden crown.

The days became months, and the months became years, until the passing of time became immeasurable. Many a mortal visited her since that awful time long ago, when she had been stripped of all she held dear, of everything that made her who she once had been.

Some came seeking shelter from the harsh mountain cold, some came for the heat of a clandestine meeting. Echo repeated them all, every word, for she had grown so lonely that she was grateful for the conversation, even if it was one-sided.

In the cruelest twist of fate, she had become the *eidolon* Narcissus had thought—hoped—her to be, left to roam the earth, going from cave to cave, for that was where she could be heard best, just to find a bit of company.

She wished she could tell them everything. How there once was a nymph who fell in love with a beautiful young man. She would explain in earnest why he could not return her love, for he had accidentally been enchanted to fall in love with his own reflection. She would recount the story of how she had tried her best to make him see her, but in the end, all had been lost, and her never-ending and resounding love for him had become nothing more than a myth.

THE END

GET A PREVIEW OF THE WEAVER AND THE WEB

Little Arachne shivered when she slipped from the warmth of her bed and into the chill of night. There was no slumber to rub from her eyes, for she had not been sleeping. She had been lying awake for hours, thinking of how she would arrange the colored threads on her mother's loom.

She crept silently to the door that separated her family's home from the shop where they sold their wares. Her heart pounded in her chest, but it was not from fear of the dark like other children. She knew these rooms and short halls like the back of her hand. No, her pulse jumped in anticipation from what she was about to do.

Of the things sold in their shop—bolts of fine cloth weaved by her mother and dyed by her father, the edges then stitched and embroidered with silk thread by her older siblings, the intricate and colorful tapestries were Arachne's favorite.

From the time she could walk on her own, Arachne was eager to learn her mother's craft. She would stare transfixed as her older siblings would comb and spin wool or wind silk threads, annoying them with her endless questions. *When would she be a weaver like mama* was the one she asked most often.

Her heart would sink every time her sister would laugh at her, telling her she wasn't old enough to sit at the loom. *Why, her feet didn't even reach the floor when she sat on the stool!* Once her brother would join in the ribbing, Arachne would run to their *mama* crying, who would always stop what she was doing to take her in her arms. She would pet Arachne's long dark hair, wiping away her tears as she gently reiterated what Arachne had already been told countless times; she was too small, too antsy, too this, and too that.

Perhaps it was being told no, or that Arachne was forbidden from doing something, but the denials only ignited a burning passion within her. She continued her relentless pursuit to become a weaver like her mother until she was finally given the task of grinding the dried plants and insects to make the dyes her father used. She would help him hang the colorful yarns and silk threads, and once they were dry, she would wind them onto the bobbins. She did this happily, watching her mother carefully as she did her work and learning what went where while she created wondrous scenes out of the threads Arachne and her father had prepared for her.

When Arachne had finally mastered spinning, dying, and winding, she was allowed to sit next to her mother and push the weft down with a wooden comb while her mother inserted the shuttle into the warp near the heddles. Arachne was quick, and it wasn't long before they fell into a rhythm, working as though they were one person with two pairs of hands.

Arachne knew she only slowed her mother down working this way, but with so many patrons coming into the shop, there was no time for her mother to oversee Arachne's work if she attempted a tapestry on her own.

She was not yet tall enough to reach the top of the loom. What if she made an error? What if the warp was too tight, or worse, too loose? They could not afford to waste the expensive wool! Those were the excuses her parents gave, even though she presented her case each morning.

"Mama, imagine having two weavers in the family!" she would say to her mother before rounding on her father, tugging on the back of his tunic as he worked. "Papa, think of how much more we could earn!"

Despite her insistence, they remained firm. "A few more years, daughter," her father would say, patting her on the head with a dye-stained hand. "Now run along. There is wool to be combed and I must get back to my work."

Arachne would sigh, always careful to hide the sullen look on her face as she completed the day's chores, which included leaving the small town in which they lived each evening and going up into the grassy mountainside to help corral her grandfather's sheep for the night. It was a rite of passage; all her siblings had taken their turn at helping the old man.

On her way there, she would let her mind wander, smiling at the vibrant scenes she saw herself weaving inside her head. She supposed she couldn't blame her parents for their trepidation. They had the shop to run. In her opinion, that was even more reason to let her weave. After all, she was twelve now, and, besides that, she had waited long enough. She *knew* she could do it.

An adolescent bird simply knows when it's time to leave the nest, does it not?

Her innate sense of knowing wasn't the problem. It was convincing her mother and father to trust her. There was no other way to prove to them she could earn her keep than to take matters into her own hands. Like a bird ready to venture out into the open sky, she had waited until her parents were not around to test her wings for the first time.

A small flickering light filled the room when Arachne lit the oil lamp and then tip-toed over to the corner where her mother weaved each day. She sat the lamp on a wooden table before inhaling deeply. Tonight, Arachne would finish the tapestry her mother had begun. In the morning, her mother and father would praise her work, and she would finally be allowed to weave on her own.

Her gaze traveled over the half-finished tapestry, darting to the places where her mother had made small errors. No matter, they would be unnoticeable soon enough. Arachne bent to pick up the shuttle, grinning at the weight of it in her hand, and as she climbed onto the stool and began to weave, her lips widened into a grin.

The Author

Forever a fan of fairytales, folklore, and mythology, Kerri brings life to the mythological characters you know and love... or love to hate.

Kerri lives in Michigan with her husband, son and cat they lovingly but aptly refer to as The Maleficence. Mel for short. If Kerri isn't raking leaves or shoveling snow, she's either reading, writing or has fled her evil to-do list and fallen down an Internet rabbit hole... Or possibly just fallen and can't get up.

For news and updates about upcoming releases, sign up for Kerri's newsletter at kerrikeberly.com. For an inside look at the day in the life of a crafty crochet-addicted, DIY-loving, Greek mythology-obsessed author, follow her on Facebook, Instagram, and TikTok.

www.ingramcontent.com/pod-product-compliance
Lightning Source LLC
Chambersburg PA
CBHW030903200726
48289CB00003B/870